818
T

218594

HENRY DAVID THOREAU

A Man for Our Time

HENRY DAVID THOREAU

A Man for Our Time

Selections and Drawings by
James Daugherty

The Viking Press   New York

To
the memory of
Hazel and Moore S. Achenbach
and
our lifelong friendship, whose warmth and
endurance has enriched my wayfaring over
so many years

Copyright © 1967 by James Daugherty
All rights reserved
First published in 1967 by The Viking Press, Inc.
625 Madison Avenue, New York, N.Y. 10022
Published simultaneously in Canada by
The Macmillan Company of Canada Limited
Library of Congress catalog card number: AC 67-10648
818   1. Thoreau—Selections
        2. American literature
Second printing March 1969

Printed in the U.S.A. by Halliday Lithograph Corporation

Contents

Introduction

When Henry David Thoreau was born in Concord in 1817, the morning sun of independence had risen brightly over Beacon Hill and Boston Common and shone gloriously on the brand-new Constitution that triumphantly held together the United States of America. The new democratic Republic was stepping out on the highroad of manifest destiny, and the sky was the limit.

As the century advanced, Thoreau would read in The Concord Freeman about wagon trains plodding fifteen miles a day across the sun-baked plains on the long trail to Oregon that had been broken by Marcus and Narcissa Whitman, of the iron horse that was pushing progress to the Mississippi, and of Yankee clipper ships that plowed the Seven Seas, bringing back exotic cargoes in their holds. When gold was discovered in California, the Argonauts of '49 crossed the continent in a wild migration in pursuit of fabulous fortunes.

The sky was the limit. Except that already a dark cloud hung ominously on the horizon and was growing ever larger — black slavery. And in 1859 John Brown surrendered to Robert E. Lee at the firehouse in Harper's Ferry and was hanged for attempting to incite a slave rebellion and to overthrow the United States government. These were pictures and processions that came and went in the light and shade of Thoreau's long thoughts as he daily walked in the woods and fields of his beloved Concord.

Concord was a village of some two thousand inhabitants, mostly farmers, situated about twenty miles west of Boston, and it was there that Henry David Thoreau was born and spent his life. As a boy he had listened to old men who had been there tell of the fight at Concord Bridge. He knew veterans who had followed Washington as he led his Continental army triumphant through the streets of Boston.

After his graduation from Harvard in 1837, Thoreau returned to his beloved village and his devoted family circle. He soon became the friend of Ralph Waldo Emerson, who had moved to Concord in 1834.

Emerson was a Boston preacher who had left his church to become a free-lance writer and lecturer. He started an intellectual revolution with his essay "Nature." His efforts to bring light and air into the musty New England theology (the Divinity College address) and academic routines (the "American scholar" oration) shocked the clergy and startled the Harvard professors. He called to young America: "Young man, obey your heart."

When Emerson moved to Concord, he attracted there a circle of passionate idealists, some of whom were geniuses. They called themselves "transcendentalists," and Thoreau became one of this group. Emerson was their prophet and his essay "Nature" their Bible. Their philosophy transcended the outer material world to explore inner meanings and the reality behind and beyond appearances. It exchanged things for thoughts.

Emerson called on American writers to create an American literature that would be native, affirmative, and original, instead of an imitation of European works. He urged writers to find their inspiration in American life and its vision of freedom and democracy.

By mid-century five books dealing with American themes appeared almost at the same time: Nathaniel Hawthorne's The Scarlet Letter in 1850; Herman Melville's Moby Dick in 1851 (the same year that Harriet Beecher Stowe's Uncle Tom's Cabin appeared serially); Thoreau's Walden in 1854; and Walt Whitman's great chant of democracy, Leaves of Grass, in 1855. The

10

Scarlet Letter *was an immediate success;* Uncle Tom's Cabin *rocked the nation and has been popular ever since.* Leaves of Grass *created a scandal,* Walden *sold a few copies, and* Moby Dick *was ignored. These writers were the prophets of the bright and enduring American dream.*

Emerson delighted in young Thoreau's independence and called him "my boy." On their long walks and talks together Henry introduced his friend to the secrets of the swamps and fields and the teeming life of stream and meadow.

Harvard graduates of that time were expected to enter the professions and become sucessful preachers, lawyers, doctors, or business tycoons, but Thoreau already knew that he wanted to be a writer and poet and independent thinker. He wasn't interested in business or making money, but planned to live simply and in his own way. His problem was how to make a living and still have time to write.

Young Thoreau found that if he lived frugally he could earn enough in a few weeks to live for a year. So he went to the woods and built a hut by Walden Pond on land that Emerson owned and permitted him to use rent free.

"I went to the woods because I wanted to live deliberately, to front only the essential facts of life, and see if I could not learn what it had to teach, and not, when I came to die, discover that I had not lived."

He bragged about how little it cost him to live and when he told Emerson at the dinner table that he had lived on twenty-seven cents the previous week, Lidian, Emerson's wife, said: "But Henry, you forget that you dined with us three times."

Nevertheless, Thoreau could always do many things well. He was at different times a carpenter, a gardener, a pencil maker, and a surveyor. He was also a scholar in ancient languages (he read Greek and Latin for pleasure), a poet, a lecturer, a naturalist. He played the flute, and was not above hiring out as a day laborer or joining in a country dance. Always he kept his daily journal, and this became the treasure house of his thoughts. From these thoughts he took his lectures, essays, and published writings. For Thoreau was above all a writer, a master of words and builder of sentences. And his writings have been read around the world, giving courage and inspiration to men—among them Gandhi and Martin Luther King—and peoples seeking freedom, independence, and justice.

Though Thoreau was not a party Abolitionist, he denounced the State of Massachusetts for obligingly returning runaway slaves to their Southern owners and offered comfort and help to exhausted slaves who came to his door on their way to freedom in Canada.

One day, while he was living at Walden Pond, Thoreau went to town to have a shoe repaired and was arrested for not paying his annual poll tax of $1.50. In fact, he had not paid it for four years, as a protest against slavery. Although "a veiled lady" paid the tax for him, he chose to spend the night in the town jail. He wrote in his essay on "Civil Disobedience": "Under a government which imprisons any unjustly, the true place for a just man is also a prison."

When John Brown came to Concord in 1857 he stayed at Thoreau's mother's boarding house. Thoreau met him there, heard his lecture at the Concord Lyceum, and became his ardent admirer and supporter. After the raid on Harper's Ferry and Brown's hanging, Thoreau spoke and wrote in Old Osawatomie's defense, proclaiming him a martyr and Christian hero.

Thoreau did not outlive Brown for long. He was a victim of consumption and bravely endured a long illness. In his last hours his aunt at his bedside asked that question always so dreadful to the Yankee soul: "Henry, have you made your peace with God?"

"I did not know that we had ever quarreled," he said.

WALDEN
Part One

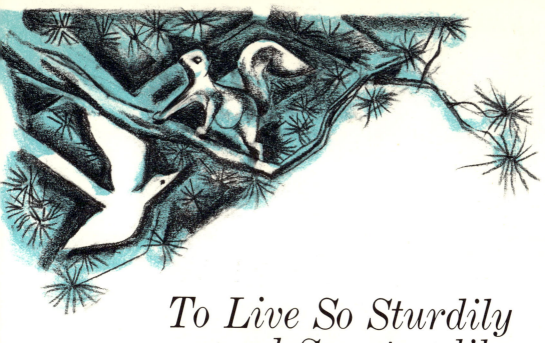

To Live So Sturdily and Spartan-like

I WENT TO THE woods because I wished to live deliberately, to front only the essential facts of life, and see if I could not learn what it had to teach, and not, when I came to die, discover that I had not lived. I did not wish to live what was not life, living is so dear; nor did I wish to practice resignation, unless it was quite necessary. I wanted to live deep and suck out all the marrow of life, to live so sturdily and Spartan-like as to put to rout all that was not life, to cut a broad swath and shave close, to drive life into a corner, and reduce it to its lowest terms, and, if it proved to be mean, why then to get the whole and genuine meanness of it, and publish its meanness to the world; or if it were sublime, to know it by experience, and be able to give a true account of it in my next excursion. For most men, it appears to me, are in a strange uncertainty about it, whether it is of the devil or of God, and have *somewhat hastily* concluded that it is the chief end of man here to "glorify God and enjoy him forever."

15

The mass of men lead lives of quiet desperation. What is called resignation is confirmed desperation. From the desperate city you go into the desperate country, and have to console yourself with the bravery of minks and muskrats.

The Cats of Zanzibar

IT IS NOT WORTH the whole to go around the world to count the cats in Zanzibar. Yet do this even till you can do better, and you may perhaps find some "Symmes' Hole" by which to get at the inside at last. England and France, Spain and Portugal, Gold Coast and Slave Coast, all front on this private sea; but no bark from them has ventured out of sight of land, though it is without doubt the direct way to India. If you would learn to speak all tongues and conform to the customs of all nations, if you would travel farther than all travelers, be naturalized in all climes, and cause the Sphinx to dash her head against a stone, even obey the precept of the old philosopher, and Explore thyself. Herein are demanded the eye and the nerve. Only the defeated and deserters go to the wars, cowards that run away and enlist. Start now on that farthest western way, which does not pause at the Mississippi or the Pacific, nor conduct toward a worn-out China or Japan, but leads on direct, a tangent to this sphere, summer and winter, day and night, sundown, moondown, and at last earth down too.

17

Infinitely Wild

OUR VILLAGE LIFE WOULD stagnate if it were not for the unexplored forests and meadows which surround it. We need the tonic of wildness—to wade sometimes in marshes where the bittern and the meadow-hen lurk, and hear the booming of the snipe; to smell the whispering sedge where only some wilder and more solitary fowl builds her nest, and the mink crawls with its belly close to the ground. At the same time that we are earnest to explore and learn all things, we require that all things be mysterious and unexplorable, that land and sea be infinitely wild, unsurveyed and unfathomed by us because unfathomable. We can never have enough of Nature. We must be refreshed by the sight of inexhaustible vigor, vast and Titanic features, the seacoast with its wrecks, the wilderness with its living and its decaying trees, the thundercloud, and the rain which lasts three weeks and produces freshets. We need to witness our own limits transgressed, and some life pasturing freely where we never wander.

19

I Love a Broad Margin to My Life

I DID NOT READ books the first summer; I hoed beans. Nay, I often did better than this. There were times when I could not afford to sacrifice the bloom of the present moment to any work, whether of the head or hands. I love a broad margin to my life. Sometimes, in a summer morning, having taken my accustomed bath, I sat in my sunny doorway from sunrise till noon, rapt in a revery, amidst the pines and hickories and sumachs, in undisturbed solitude and stillness, while the birds sang around or flitted noiseless through the house, until by the sun falling in at my west window, or the noise of some traveler's wagon on the distant highway, I was reminded of the lapse of time. I grew in those seasons like corn in the night, and they were far better than any work of the hands would have been. They were not time subtracted from my life, but so much over and above my usual allowance. I realized what the Orientals mean by contemplation and the forsaking of works. For the most part, I minded not how the hours went. The day advanced as if to light some work of mine; it was morning, and lo, now it is evening, and nothing memorable is accomplished. Instead of singing like the birds, I silently smiled at my incessant good fortune.

The Village of Noblemen

IN THIS COUNTRY, THE village should in some respects take the place of the nobleman of Europe. It should be the patron of the fine arts. It is rich enough. It wants only the magnanimity and refinement. It can spend money enough on such things as farmers and traders value, but it is thought Utopian to propose spending money for things which more intelligent men know to be of far more worth. . . . As the nobleman of cultivated taste surrounds himself with whatever conduces to his culture: genius—learning—wit—books—paintings—statuary—music —philosophical instruments, and the like; so let the village do—not stop short at a pedagogue, a parson, a sexton, a parish library, and three selectmen, because our pilgrim forefathers got through a cold winter once on a bleak rock with these. . . . Instead of noblemen, let us have noble villages of men. If it is necessary, omit one bridge over the river, go round a little there, and throw one arch at least over the darker gulf of ignorance which surrounds us.

22

Follow Your Genius

I HAD THIS ADVANTAGE, at least, in my mode of life, over those who were obliged to look abroad for amusement, to society and the theater, that my life itself was become my amusement and never ceased to be novel. It was a drama of many scenes and without an end. If we were always indeed getting our living, and regulating our lives according to the last and best mode we had learned, we should never be troubled with ennui. Follow your genius closely enough, and it will not fail to show you a fresh prospect every hour. Housework was a pleasant pastime. When my floor was dirty, I rose early, and, setting all my furniture out of doors on the grass, bed and bedstead making but one budget, dashed water on the floor, and sprinkled white sand from the pond on it, and then with a broom scrubbed it clean and white; and by the time the villagers had broken their fast the morning sun had dried my house sufficiently to allow me to move in again, and my meditations were almost uninterrupted. It was pleasant to see my whole household effects out on the grass, making a little pile like a gypsy's pack, and my three-legged table, from which I did not remove the books and pen and ink, standing amid the pines and hickories. They seemed glad to get out themselves, and as if unwilling to be brought in. I was sometimes tempted to stretch an awning over them and take my seat there. It was worth the while to see the sun shine on these things, and hear the free wind blow on them; so much more interesting most familiar objects look out of doors than in the house. A bird sits on the next bough, life-everlasting grows under the table, and blackberry vines run round its legs; pine cones, chestnut burs, and strawberry leaves are strewn about. It looked as if this was the way these forms came to be transferred to our furniture, to tables, chairs, and bedsteads—because they once stood in their midst.

My House

THE NORTH WIND HAD already begun to cool the pond, though it took many weeks of steady blowing to accomplish it, it is so deep. When I began to have a fire at evening, before I plastered my house, the chimney carried smoke particularly well, because of the numerous chinks between the boards. Yet I passed some cheerful evenings in that cool and airy apartment, surrounded by the rough brown boards full of knots, and rafters with the bark on high overhead. My house never pleased my eye so much after it was plastered, though I was obliged to confess that it was more comfortable. Should not every apartment in which man dwells be lofty enough to create some obscurity overhead, where flickering shadows may play at evening about the rafters? These forms are more agreeable to the fancy and imagination than fresco paintings or other the most expensive furniture. I now first began to inhabit my house, I may say, when I began to use it for warmth as well as shelter. I had got a couple of old firedogs to keep the wood from the hearth, and it did me good to see the soot form on the back of the chimney which I had built, and I poked the fire with more right and more satisfaction than usual. My dwelling was small, and I could hardly entertain an echo in it; but it seemed larger for being a single apartment and remote from neighbors. All the attractions of a house were concentrated in one room; it was kitchen, chamber, parlor, and keeping-room; and whatever satisfaction parent or child, master or servant, derive from living in a house, I enjoyed it all. Cato says, the master of a family (*patremfamilias*) must have in his rustic villa "*cellam oleariam, vinariam, dolia multa, uti lubeat caritatem expectare, et rei, et virtuti, et gloriae erit*," that is, "an oil and wine cellar, many casks, so that it may be pleasant to expect hard times; it will be for his advantage, and virtue, and glory." I had in my cellar a firkin of potatoes, about two quarts of peas with the weevil in them, and on my shelf a little rice, a jug of molasses, and of rye and Indian meal a peck each.

Morning

EVERY MORNING WAS A cheerful invitation to make my life of equal simplicity, and I may say innocence, with Nature herself. I have been as sincere a worshiper of Aurora as the Greeks. I got up early and bathed in the pond; that was a religious exercise, and one of the best things which I did. They say that characters were engraven on the bathing tub of King Tching-thang to this effect: "Renew thyself completely each day; do it again, and again, and forever again." I can understand that. Morning brings back the heroic ages. I was as much affected by the faint hum of a mosquito making its invisible and unimaginable tour through my apartment at earliest dawn, when I was sitting with door and windows open, as I could be by any trumpet that ever sang of fame. It was Homer's requiem; itself an Iliad and Odyssey in the air, singing its own wrath and wanderings. There was something cosmical about it; a standing advertisement, till forbidden, of the everlasting vigor and fertility of the world. The morning, which is the most memorable season of the day, is the awakening hour. Then there is least somnolence in us; and for an hour, at least, some part of us awakes which slumbers all the rest of the day and night. Little is to be expected of that day, if it can be called a day, to which we are not awakened by our Genius, but by the mechanical nudgings of some servitor, are not awakened by our own newly acquired force and aspirations from within, accompanied by the undulations of celestial music, instead of factory bells, and a fragrance filling the air—to a higher life than we fell asleep from; and thus the darkness bear its fruit, and prove itself to be good, no less than the light. That man who does not believe that each day contains an earlier, more sacred and auroral hour than he has yet profaned, has despaired of life, and is pursuing a descending and darkening way. After a partial cessation of his sensuous life, the soul of man, or its organs rather, are reinvigorated each day, and his Genius tries again what noble life it can make. All memorable events, I should say, transpire in morning time and in a morning atmosphere. The Vedas say, "All intelligences awake with the morning." Poetry and art, and the fairest and most memorable of the actions of men, date from such an hour. All poets and heroes, like Memnon, are the children of Aurora, and emit their

28

music at sunrise. To him whose elastic and vigorous thought keeps pace with the sun, the day is a perpetual morning. It matters not what the clocks say or the attitudes and labors of men. Morning is when I am awake and there is a dawn in me. Moral reform is the effort to throw off sleep. Why is it that men give so poor an account of their day if they have not been slumbering? They are not such poor calculators. If they had not been overcome with drowsiness they would have performed something. The millions are awake enough for physical labor; but only one in a million is awake enough for effective intellectual exertion, only one in a hundred millions to a poetic or divine life. To be awake is to be alive. I have never yet met a man who was quite awake. How could I have looked him in the face?

The Spring

IT IS REMARKABLE HOW many creatures live wild and free
though secret in the woods, and still sustain themselves in the
neighborhood of towns, suspected by hunters only. How retired
the otter manages to live here! He grows to be four feet long, as
big as a small boy, perhaps without any human being getting
a glimpse of him. I formerly saw the raccoon in the woods
behind where my house is built, and probably still heard their
whinnering at night. Commonly I rested an hour or two in the
shade at noon, after planting, and ate my lunch, and read a
little by a spring which was the source of a swamp and of a
brook, oozing from under Brister's Hill, half a mile from my
field. The approach to this was through a succession of descending grassy hollows, full of young pitch pines, into a larger wood
about the swamp. There, in a very secluded and shaded spot,
under a spreading white pine, there was yet a clean firm sward
to sit on. I had dug out the spring and made a well of clear gray
water, where I could dip up a pailful without roiling it, and
thither I went for this purpose almost every day in mid-sum-
mer, when the pond was warmest. Thither too the woodcock
led her brood, to probe the mud for worms, flying but a foot
above them down the bank, while they ran in a troop beneath;
but at last, spying me, she would leave her young and circle
round and round me, nearer and nearer till within four or five
feet, pretending broken wings and legs, to attract my attention, and get off her young, who would already have taken up
their march, with faint wiry peep, single file through the

30

swamp, as she directed. Or I heard the peep of the young when I could not see the parent bird. There too the turtle-doves sat over the spring, or fluttered from bough to bough of the soft white pines over my head; or the red squirrel, coursing down the nearest bough, was particularly familiar and inquisitive. You only need sit still long enough in some attractive spot in the woods that all its inhabitants may exhibit themselves to you by turns.

The Bean Field

MEANWHILE MY BEANS, THE length of whose rows, added together, was seven miles already planted, were impatient to be hoed, for the earliest had grown considerably before the latest were in the ground; indeed they were not easily to be put off. What was the meaning of this so steady and self-respecting, this small Herculean labor, I knew not. I came to love my rows, my beans, though so many more than I wanted. They attached me to the earth, and so I got strength like Antaeus. But why should I raise them? Only Heaven knows. This was my curious labor all summer—to make this portion of the earth's surface, which had yielded only cinquefoil, blackberries, johnswort, and the like, before, sweet wild fruits and pleasant flowers, produce instead this pulse. What shall I learn of beans or beans of me? I cherish them, I hoe them, early and late I have an eye to them; and this is my day's work. It is a fine broad leaf to look on. My auxiliaries are the dews and rains which water this dry soil, and what fertility is in the soil itself, which for the most part is lean and effete. My enemies are worms, cool days, and most of all woodchucks. The last have nibbled for me a quarter of an acre clean. But what right had I to oust johnswort and the rest, and break up their ancient herb garden? Soon, however, the remaining beans will be too tough for them, and go forward to meet new foes.

Never Lonesome

SOMETIMES, WHEN I COMPARE myself with other men, it seems as if I were more favored by the gods than they, beyond any deserts that I am conscious of; as if I had a warrant and surety at their hands which my fellows have not, and were especially guided and guarded. I do not flatter myself, but if it be possible they flatter me. I have never felt lonesome, or in the least oppressed by a sense of solitude, but once, and that was a few weeks after I came to the woods, when, for an hour, I doubted if the near neighborhood of man was not essential to a serene and healthy life. To be alone was something unpleasant. But I was at the same time conscious of a slight insanity in my mood, and seemed to foresee my recovery. In the midst of a gentle rain while these thoughts prevailed, I was suddenly sensible of such sweet and beneficent society in Nature, in the very pattering of the drops, and in every sound and sight around my house, an infinite and unaccountable friendliness all at once like an atmosphere sustaining me, as made the fancied advantages of human neighborhood insignificant, and I have never thought of them since. Every little pine needle expanded and swelled with sympathy and befriended me. I was so distinctly made aware of the presence of something kindred to me, even in scenes which we are accustomed to call wild and dreary, and also that the nearest of blood to me and humanest was not a person nor a villager, that I thought no place could ever be strange to me again.

Drifting

WHEN I FIRST PADDLED a boat on Walden, it was completely surrounded by thick and lofty pine and oak woods, and in some of its coves grape vines had run over the trees next the water and formed bowers under which a boat could pass. The hills which form its shores are so steep, and the woods on them were then so high, that, as you looked down from the west end, it had the appearance of an amphitheater for some kind of sylvan spectacle. I have spent many an hour, when I was younger, floating over its surface as the zephyr willed, having paddled my boat to the middle, and lying on my back across the seats, in a summer forenoon, dreaming awake, until I was aroused by the boat touching the sand, and I arose to see what shore my fates had impelled me to; days when idleness was the most attractive and productive industry. Many a forenoon have I stolen away, preferring to spend thus the most valued part of the day; for I was rich, if not in money, in sunny hours and summer days, and spent them lavishly; nor do I regret that I did not waste more of them in the workshop or the teacher's desk. But since I left those shores the woodchoppers have still further laid them waste, and now for many a year there will be no more rambling through the aisles of the wood, with occasional vistas through which you see the water. My Muse may be excused if she is silent henceforth. How can you expect the birds to sing when their groves are cut down?

The Axe

THE WATER IS SO transparent that the bottom can easily be discerned at the depth of twenty-five or thirty feet. Paddling over it, you may see many feet beneath the surface the schools of perch and shiners, perhaps only an inch long, yet the former easily distinguished by their transverse bars, and you think that they must be ascetic fish that find a subsistence there. Once, in the winter, many years ago, when I had been cutting holes through the ice in order to catch pickerel, as I stepped ashore I tossed my axe back onto the ice, but, as if some evil genius had directed it, it slid four or five rods directly into one of the holes, where the water was twenty-five feet deep. Out of curiosity, I lay down on the ice and looked through the hole, until I saw the axe a little on one side, standing on its head, with its helve erect and gently swaying to and fro with the pulse of the pond; and there it might have stood erect and swaying till in the course of time the handle rotted off, if I had not disturbed it. Making another hole directly over it with an ice chisel which I had, and cutting down the longest birch which I could find in the neighborhood with my knife, I made a slip noose, which I attached to its end, and, letting it down carefully, passed it over the knob of the handle, and drew it by a line along the birch, and so pulled the axe out again.

Little Reading

I THINK THAT HAVING learned our letters we should read the best that is in literature, and not be forever repeating our a b abs, and words of one syllable, in the fourth or fifth classes, sitting on the lowest and foremost form all our lives. Most men are satisfied if they read or hear read, and perchance have been convicted by the wisdom of one good book, the Bible, and for the rest of their lives vegetate and dissipate their faculties in what is called easy reading. There is a work in several volumes in our Circulating Library entitled Little Reading, which I thought referred to a town of that name which I had not been to. . . .

The best books are not read even by those who are called good readers. What does our Concord culture amount to? There is in this town, with a very few exceptions, no taste for the best or for very good books even in English literature, whose words all can read and spell. Even the college-bred and so-called liberally educated men here and elsewhere have really little or no acquaintance with the English classics; and as for the recorded wisdom of mankind, the ancient classics and Bibles, which are accessible to all who will know of them, there are the feeblest efforts anywhere made to become acquainted with them. . . . One who has just come from reading perhaps one of the best English books will find how many with whom he can converse about it? Or suppose he comes from reading a Greek or Latin classic in the original, whose praises are familiar even to the so-called illiterate; he will find nobody at all to speak to, but must keep silence about it. Indeed, there is hardly the professor in our colleges, who, if he has mastered the difficulties of the language, has proportionally mastered the difficulties of the wit and poetry of a Greek poet, and has any sympathy to impart to the alert and heroic reader; and as for the sacred Scriptures, or Bibles of mankind, who in this town can tell me even their titles? Most men do not know that any nation but the Hebrews have had a scripture. A man, any man, will go considerably out of his way to pick up a silver dollar; but here are golden words, which the wisest men of antiquity have uttered, and whose worth the wise of every succeeding age have assured us of; and yet we learn to read only as far as Easy Reading, the primers and classbooks, and when we leave school, the "Little Reading," and storybooks, which are for boys and beginners; and our reading, our conversation and thinking, are all on a very low level, worthy only of pygmies and manikins.

Solitude

THIS IS A DELICIOUS evening, when the whole body is one sense, and imbibes delight through every pore. I go and come with a strange liberty in Nature, a part of herself. As I walk along the stony shore of the pond in my shirt sleeves, though it is cool as well as cloudy and windy, and I see nothing special to attract me, all the elements are unusually congenial to me. The bull-frogs trump to usher in the night, and the note of the whippoor-will is borne on the rippling wind from over the water. Sympathy with the fluttering alder and poplar leaves almost takes away my breath; yet, like the lake, my serenity is rippled but not ruffled. These small waves raised by the evening wind are as remote from storm as the smooth reflecting surface. Though it is now dark, the wind still blows and roars in the wood, the waves still dash, and some creatures lull the rest with their notes. The repose is never complete. The wildest animals do not repose, but seek their prey now; the fox, and skunk, and rabbit, now roam the fields and woods without fear. They are Nature's watchmen—links which connect the days of animated life.

The Lost Bottom

AS I WAS DESIROUS to recover the long lost bottom of Walden Pond, I surveyed it carefully, before the ice broke up, early in '46, with compass and chain and sounding line. There have been many stories told about the bottom, or rather no bottom, of this pond, which certainly had no foundation for themselves. It is remarkable how long men will believe in the bottomlessness of a pond without taking the trouble to sound it. I have visited two such Bottomless Ponds in one walk in this neighborhood. Many have believed that Walden reached quite through to the other side of the globe. Some who have lain flat on the ice for a long time, looking down through the illusive medium, perchance with watery eyes into the bargain, and driven to hasty conclusions by the fear of catching cold in their breasts, have seen vast holes "into which a load of hay might be driven," if there were anybody to drive it, the undoubted source of the Styx and entrance to the Infernal Regions from these parts. Others have gone down from the village with a "fifty-six" and a wagon-load of inch rope, but yet have failed to find any bottom; for while the "fifty-six" was resting by the way, they were paying out the rope in the vain attempt to fathom their truly immeasurable capacity for marvelousness. But I can assure my readers that Walden has a reasonably tight bottom at a not unreasonable, though at an unusual, depth. I fathomed it easily with a cod-line and a stone weighing about a pound and a half, and could tell accurately when the stone left the bottom, by having to pull so much harder before the water got underneath to help me. The greatest depth was exactly one hundred and two feet; to which may be added the five feet which it has risen since, making one hundred and seven. This is a remarkable depth for so small an area; yet not an inch of it can be spared by the imagination. What if all ponds were shallow? Would it not react on the minds of men? I am thankful that this pond was made deep and pure for a symbol. While men believe in the infinite some ponds will be thought to be bottomless.

Midnight Fishing

SOMETIMES, AFTER STAYING IN a village parlor till the family had all retired, I have returned to the woods, and, partly with a view to the next day's dinner, spent the hours of midnight fishing from a boat by moonlight, serenaded by owls and foxes, and hearing, from time to time, the creaking note of some unknown bird close at hand. These experiences were very memorable and valuable to me, anchored in forty feet of water, and twenty or thirty rods from the shore, surrounded sometimes by thousands of small perch and shiners, dimpling the surface with their tails in the moonlight, and communicating by a long flaxen line with mysterious nocturnal fishes which had their dwelling forty feet below, or sometimes dragging sixty feet of line about the pond as I drifted in the gentle night breeze, now and then feeling a slight vibration along it, indicative of some life prowling about its extremity, of dull uncertain blundering purpose there, and slow to make up its mind. At length you slowly raise, pulling hand over hand, some horned pout squeaking and squirming to the upper air. It was very queer, especially in dark nights, when your thoughts had wandered to vast and cosmogonal themes in other spheres, to feel this faint jerk, which came to interrupt your dreams and link you to Nature again. It seemed as if I might next cast my line upward into the air, as well as downward into this element, which was scarcely more dense. Thus I caught two fishes as it were with one hook.

Rainbow over
My Shoulder

As I was leaving the Irishman's roof after the rain, bending
my steps again to the pond, my haste to catch pickerel, wading
in retired meadows, in sloughs and bogholes, in forlorn and

savage places, appeared for an instant trivial to me who had
been sent to school and college; but as I ran down the hill
toward the reddening west, with the rainbow over my shoulder,
and some faint tinkling sounds borne to my ear through the
cleansed air, from I know not what quarter, my Good Genius
seemed to say, Go fish and hunt far and wide day by day—
farther and wider—and rest thee by many brooks and hearth-
sides without misgiving. Remember thy Creator in the days of
thy youth. Rise free from care before the dawn, and seek ad-
ventures. Let the noon find thee by other lakes, and the night
overtake thee everywhere at home. There are no larger fields
than these, no worthier games than may here be played. Grow
wild according to thy nature, like these sedges and brakes,
which will never become English hay. Let the thunder rumble;
what if it threaten ruin to farmers' crops? that is not its errand
to thee. Take shelter under the cloud, while they flee to carts
and sheds. Let not to get a living be thy trade, but thy sport.
Enjoy the land, but own it not. Through want of enterprise and
faith men are where they are, buying and selling, and spending
their lives like serfs.

Girls and Boys

I COULD NOT BUT notice some of the peculiarities of my visitors. Girls and boys and young women generally seemed glad to be in the woods. They looked in the pond and at the flowers, and improved their time. Men of business, even farmers, thought only of solitude and employment, and of the great distance at which I dwelt from something or other; and though they said that they loved a ramble in the woods occasionally, it was obvious that they did not. Restless committed men, whose time was all taken up in getting a living or keeping it; ministers who spoke of God as if they enjoyed a monopoly of the subject, who could not bear all kinds of opinions; doctors, lawyers, uneasy housekeepers who pried into my cupboard and bed when I was out—how came Mrs. ——— to know that my sheets were not as clean as hers?—young men who had ceased to be young, and had concluded that it was safest to follow the beaten track of the professions—all these generally said that it was not possible to do so much good in my position. Ay! there was the rub. The old and infirm and the timid, of whatever age or sex, thought most of sickness, and sudden accident and death; to them life seemed full of danger—what danger is there if you don't think of any?—and they thought that a prudent man would carefully select the safest position, where Dr. B. might be on hand at a moment's warning. To them the village was literally a *com-munity*, a league for mutual defense, and you would suppose that they would not go a-huckleberrying without a medicine chest. The amount of it is, if a man is alive,

there is always *danger* that he may die, though the danger must
be allowed to be less in proportion as he is dead-and-alive to
begin with. A man sits as many risks as he runs. Finally, there
were the self-styled reformers, the greatest bores of all, who
thought that I was forever singing,

> This is the house that I built;
> This is the man that lives in the house that I built;

but they did not know that the third line was,

> These are the folks that worry the man
> That lives in the house that I built.

I did not fear the hen-harriers, for I kept no chickens; but I
feared the men-harriers rather.

I had more cheering visitors than the last. Children come a-
berrying, railroad men taking a Sunday morning walk in clean
shirts, fishermen and hunters, poets and philosophers; in short,
all honest pilgrims, who came out to the woods for freedom's
sake, and really left the village behind, I was ready to greet
with, "Welcome, Englishmen! Welcome, Englishmen!" for I
had had communication with that race.

A Little
Stardust Caught

IF THE DAY AND the night are such that you greet them with joy, and life emits a fragrance like flowers and sweet-scented herbs, is more elastic, more starry, more immortal—that is your success. All nature is your congratulation, and you have cause momentarily to bless yourself. The greatest gains and values are farthest from being appreciated. We easily come to doubt if they exist. We soon forget them. They are the highest reality. Perhaps the facts most astounding and most real are never communicated by man to man. The true harvest of my daily life is somewhat as intangible and indescribable as the tints of morning or evening. It is a little stardust caught, a segment of the rainbow which I have clutched.

Yet, for my part, I was never unusually squeamish; I could sometimes eat a fried rat with a good relish, if it were necessary. I am glad to have drunk water so long, for the same reason that I prefer the natural sky to an opium-eater's heaven. I would fain keep sober always; and there are infinite degrees of drunkenness. I believe that water is the only drink for a wise man; wine is not so noble a liquor; and think of dashing the hopes of a morning with a cup of warm coffee, or of an evening with a dish of tea! Ah, how low I fall when I am tempted by them! Even music may be intoxicating. Such apparently slight causes destroyed Greece and Rome, and will destroy England and America. Of all ebriosity, who does not prefer to be intoxicated by the air he breathes?

The Half-wit

ONE DAY, IN PARTICULAR, an inoffensive, simple-minded pauper, whom with others I had often seen used as fencing stuff, standing or sitting on a bushel in the fields to keep cattle and himself from straying, visited me, and expressed a wish to live as I did. He told me, with the utmost simplicity and truth, quite superior, or rather *inferior*, to anything that is called humility, that he was "deficient in intellect." These were his words. The Lord had made him so, yet he supposed the Lord cared as much for him as for another. "I have always been so," said he, "from my childhood; I never had much mind; I was not like other children; I am weak in the head. It was the Lord's will, I suppose." And there he was to prove the truth of his words. He was a metaphysical puzzle to me. I have rarely met a fellow-man on such promising ground—it was so simple and sincere and so true, all that he said. And, true enough, in proportion as he appeared to humble himself was he exalted. I did not know at first but it was the result of a wise policy. It seemed that from such a basis of truth and frankness as the poor weakheaded pauper had laid, our intercourse might go forward to something better than the intercourse of sages. . . .

Men of almost every degree of wit called on me in the migrating season. Some who had more wits than they knew what to do with; run-away slaves with plantation manners, who listened from time to time, like the fox in the fable, as if they heard the hounds a-baying on their track, and looked at me beseechingly, as much as to say,

"O Christian, will you send me back?"

50

Bronson Alcott

I SHOULD NOT FORGET that during my last winter at the pond there was another welcome visitor, who at one time came through the village, through snow and rain and darkness, till he saw my lamp through the trees, and shared with me some long winter evenings. One of the last of the philosophers—Connecticut gave him to the world—he peddled first her wares, afterwards, as he declares, his brains. These he peddles still, prompting God and disgracing man, bearing for fruit his brain only, like the nut its kernel. I think that he must be the man of the most faith of any alive. His words and attitude always suppose a better state of things than other men are acquainted with, and he will be the last man to be disappointed as the ages revolve. He has no venture in the present. But though comparatively disregarded now, when his day comes, laws unsuspected by most will take effect, and masters of families and rulers will come to him for advice. "How blind that cannot see serenity!"

52

A true friend of man; almost the only friend of human progress. An Old Mortality, say rather an Immortality, with unwearied patience and faith making plain the image engraven in men's bodies, the God of whom they are but defaced and leaning monuments. With his hospitable intellect he embraces children, beggars, insane, and scholars, and entertains the thought of all, adding to it commonly some breadth and elegance. I think that he should keep a caravansary on the world's highway, where philosophers of all nations might put up, and on his sign should be printed, "Entertainment for man, but not for his beast. Enter ye that have leisure and a quiet mind, who earnestly seek the right road." He is perhaps the sanest man and has the fewest crotchets of any I chance to know; the same yesterday and tomorrow. Of yore we had sauntered and talked, and effectually put the world behind us; for he was pledged to no institution in it, freeborn, *ingenuus*. Whichever way we turned, it seemed that the heavens and the earth had met together, since he enhanced the beauty of the landscape. A blue-robed man, whose fittest roof is the overarching sky which reflects his serenity. I do not see how he can ever die; Nature cannot spare him.

Having each some shingles of thought well dried, we sat and whittled them, trying our knives, and admiring the clear yellowish grain of the pumpkin pine. We waded so gently and reverently, or we pulled together so smoothly, that the fishes of thought were not scared from the stream, nor feared any angler on the bank, but came and went grandly, like the clouds which float through the western sky, and the mother-o'-pearl flocks which sometimes form and dissolve there. There we worked, revising mythology, rounding a fable here and there, and building castles in the air for which earth offered no worthy foundation. Great Looker! Greater Expecter! to converse with whom was a New England Night's Entertainment.

Chastity

CHASTITY IS THE FLOWERING of man; and what are called Genius, Heroism, Holiness, and the like, are but various fruits which succeed it. Man flows at once to God when the channel of purity is open. By turns our purity inspires and our impurity casts us down. He is blessed who is assured that the animal is dying out in him day by day, and the divine being established. Perhaps there is none but has cause for shame on account of the inferior and brutish nature to which he is allied. I fear that we are such gods or demigods only as fauns and satyrs, the divine allied to beasts, the creatures of appetite, and that, to some extent, our very life is our disgrace.

All sensuality is one, though it takes many forms; all purity is one. It is the same whether a man eat, or drink, or cohabit, or sleep sensually. They are but one appetite, and we only need to see a person do any one of these things to know how great a sensualist he is. The impure can neither stand nor sit with purity. When the reptile is attacked at one mouth of his burrow, he shows himself at another. If you would be chaste, you must be temperate. What is chastity? How shall a man know if he is chaste? He shall not know it. We have heard of this virtue, but we know not what it is. We speak comfortably to the rumor which we have heard. From exertion come wisdom and purity; from sloth ignorance and sensuality. In the student sensuality is a sluggish habit of mind. An unclean person is universally a slothful one, one who sits by a stove, whom the sun shines on prostrate, who reposes without being fatigued. If you would

avoid uncleanness, and all the sins, work earnestly, though it be at cleaning a stable. Nature is hard to be overcome, but she must be overcome. What avails it that you are Christian, if you are not purer than the heathen, if you deny yourself no more, if you are not more religious? I know of many systems of religion esteemed heathenish whose precepts fill the reader with shame, and provoke him to new endeavors, though it be to the performance of rites merely.

I hesitate to say these things, but it is not because of the subject—I care not how obscene my *words* are—but because I cannot speak of them without betraying my impurity. We discourse freely without shame of one form of sensuality, and are silent about another. We are so degraded that we cannot speak simply of the necessary functions of human nature. In earlier ages, in some countries, every function was reverently spoken of and regulated by law. Nothing was too trivial for the Hindu lawgiver, however offensive it may be to modern taste. He teaches how to eat, drink, cohabit, void excrement and urine, and the like, elevating what is mean, and does not falsely excuse himself by calling these things trifles.

Every man is the builder of a temple, called his body, to the god he worships, after a style purely his own, nor can he get off by hammering marble instead. We are all sculptors and painters, and our material is our own flesh and blood and bones. Any nobleness begins at once to refine a man's features, any meanness or sensuality to imbrute them.

My Mouse

THE MICE WHICH HAUNTED my house were not the common ones, which are said to have been introduced into the country, but a wild native kind not found in the village. I sent one to a distinguished naturalist, and it interested him much. When I was building, one of these had its nest underneath the house, and before I had laid the second floor, and swept out the shavings, would come out regularly at lunch time and pick up the crumbs at my feet. It probably had never seen a man before; and it soon became quite familiar, and would run over my shoes and up my clothes. It could readily ascend the sides of the room by short impulses, like a squirrel, which it resembled in its motions. At length, as I leaned with my elbow on the bench one day, it ran up my clothes, and along my sleeve, and round and round the paper which held my dinner, while I kept the latter close, and dodged and played at bo-peep with it; and when at last I held still a piece of cheese between my thumb and finger, it came and nibbled it, sitting in my hand, and afterward cleaned its face and paws, like a fly, and walked away.

57

The Red and the Black

I WAS WITNESS TO events of a less peaceful character. One day when I went out to my wood pile, or rather my pile of stumps, I observed two large ants, the one red, the other much larger, nearly half an inch long, and black, fiercely contending with one another. Having once got hold they never let go, but struggled and wrestled and rolled on the chips incessantly. Looking farther, I was surprised to find that the chips were covered with such combatants, that it was not a *duellum*, but a *bellum*, a war between two races of ants, the red always pitted against the black, and frequently two red ones to one black. The legions of these Myrmidons covered all the hills and vales in my wood-yard, and the ground was already strewn with the dead and dying, both red and black. It was the only battle which I have ever witnessed, the only battlefield I ever trod while the battle was raging; internecine war; the red republicans on the one hand, and the black imperialists on the other. On every side they were engaged in deadly combat, yet without any noise that I could hear, and human soldiers never fought so resolutely. I watched a couple that were fast locked in each other's embraces, in a little sunny valley amid the chips, now at noonday prepared to fight till the sun went down, or life went out. The smaller red champion had fastened himself like a vice to his adversary's front, and through all the tumblings on that field never for an instant ceased to gnaw at one of his feelers near the root, having already caused the other to go by the board; while the stronger black one dashed him from side to side, and, as I saw on looking nearer, had already divested him of several of his members. They fought with more pertinacity than bull-dogs. Neither manifested the least disposition to retreat. It was evident that their battle-cry was Conquer or die. In the meanwhile there came along a single red ant on the hillside of this valley, evidently full of excitement, who either had despatched his foe, or had not yet taken part in the battle; probably the latter, for he had lost none of his limbs; whose mother had charged him to return with his shield or upon it. Or perchance he was some Achilles, who had nourished his wrath apart, and had now come to avenge or rescue his Patroclus. He saw this unequal combat from afar—for the blacks were nearly twice the size of the red—he drew near with rapid pace till he stood on his guard within half an inch of the combatants; then, watching his opportunity, he sprang upon the black warrior, and commenced his operations near the root of his right foreleg, leaving the foe to select among his own members; and so there were three united for life, as if a new kind of attraction had been invented which put all other locks and cements to shame. I should not have wondered by this time to find that they had their respective musical bands stationed on some eminent chip, and playing their national airs the while, to excite the slow and cheer the dying combatants. I was myself excited somewhat even as if they had been men. The more you think of it, the less the difference. And certainly there is not the fight recorded in Concord history, at least, if in the history of America, that will bear a moment's comparison with this, whether for the numbers engaged in it, or for the patriotism and heroism displayed. For numbers and for carnage it was an Austerlitz or Dresden. Concord Fight! Two killed on the patriots' side, and

Luther Blanchard wounded! Why here every ant was a But-
trick—"Fire! for God's sake fire!"—and thousands shared the
fate of Davis and Hosmer. There was not one hireling there. I
have no doubt that it was a principle they fought for, as much
as our ancestors, and not to avoid a three-penny tax on their
tea; and the results of this battle will be as important and
memorable to those whom it concerns as those of the battle of
Bunker Hill, at least.

I took up the chip on which the three I have particularly
described were struggling, carried it into my house, and placed

it under a tumbler on my window sill, in order to see the issue. Holding a microscope to the first-mentioned red ant, I saw that, though he was assiduously gnawing at the near foreleg of his enemy, having severed his remaining feeler, his own breast was all torn away, exposing what vitals he had there to the jaws of the black warrior, whose breastplate was apparently too thick for him to pierce; and the dark carbuncles of the sufferer's eyes shone with ferocity such as war only could excite. They struggled half an hour longer under the tumbler, and when I looked again the black soldier had severed the heads of his foes from their bodies, and the still living heads were hanging on either side of him like ghastly trophies at his saddle-bow, still apparently as firmly fastened as ever, and he was endeavoring with feeble struggles, being without feelers and with only the remnant of a leg, and I know not how many other wounds, to divest himself of them; which at length, after half an hour more, he accomplished. I raised the glass, and he went off over the window sill in that crippled state. Whether he finally survived that combat, and spent the remainder of his days in some Hotel des Invalides, I do not know; but I thought that his industry would not be worth much thereafter. I never learned which party was victorious, nor the cause of the war; but I felt for the rest of that day as if I had had my feelings excited and harrowed by witnessing the struggle, the ferocity and carnage, of a human battle before my door.

The Red Squirrels

USUALLY THE RED SQUIRREL (*Sciurus Hudsonius*) waked me in the dawn, coursing over the roof and up and down the sides of the house, as if sent out of the woods for this purpose. In the course of the winter I threw out half a bushel of ears of sweet corn, which had not got ripe, onto the snow crust by my door, and was amused by watching the motions of the various animals which were baited by it. In the twilight and the night

63

the rabbits came regularly and made a hearty meal. All day long the red squirrels came and went, and afforded me much entertainment by their maneuvers. One would approach at first warily through the shrub-oaks, running over the snow crust by fits and starts like a leaf blown by the wind, now a few paces this way, with wonderful speed and waste of energy, making inconceivable haste with his "trotters," as if it were for a wager, and now as many paces that way, but never getting on more than half a rod at a time; and then suddenly pausing with a ludicrous expression and a gratuitous somerset, as if all the eyes in the universe were fixed on him—for all the motions of a squirrel, even in the most solitary recesses of the forest, imply spectators as much as those of a dancing girl—wasting more time in delay and circumspection than would have sufficed to walk the whole distance—I never saw one walk—and then suddenly, before you could say Jack Robinson, he would be in the top of a young pitch pine, winding up his clock and chiding all imaginary spectators, soliloquizing and talking to all the universe at the same time—for no reason that I could ever detect, or he himself was aware of, I suspect. At length he would reach the corn, and selecting a suitable ear, frisk about in the same uncertain trigonometrical way to the topmost stick of my woodpile, before my window, where he looked me in the face, and there sit for hours, supplying himself with a new ear from time to time, nibbling at first voraciously and throwing the half-naked cobs about; till at length he grew more dainty still and played with his food, tasting only the inside of the kernel, and the ear, which was held balanced over the stick by one paw, slipped from his careless grasp and fell to the ground, when he would look over at it with a ludicrous expression of uncertainty, as if suspecting that it had life, with a mind not made up whether to get it again, or a new one, or be off; now thinking of corn, then listening to hear what was in the wind.

So the little impudent fellow would waste many an ear in a forenoon; till at last, seizing some longer and plumper one, considerably bigger than himself, and skillfully balancing it, he would set out with it to the woods, like a tiger with a buffalo, by the same zigzag course and frequent pauses, scratching along with it as if it were too heavy for him and falling all the while, making its fall a diagonal between a perpendicular and horizontal, being determined to put it through at any rate—a singularly frivolous and whimsical fellow—and so he would get off with it to where he lived, perhaps carry it to the top of a pine tree forty or fifty rods distant, and I would afterwards find the cobs strewn about the woods in various directions.

I Rejoice
There Are Owls

I REJOICE THAT THERE are owls. Let them do the idiotic and
maniacal hooting for men. It is a sound admirably suited to
swamps and twilight woods which no day illustrates, suggest-
ing a vast and undeveloped nature which men have not recog-
nized. They represent the stark twilight and unsatisfied
thoughts which all have. All day the sun has shone on the surface of some savage swamp, where the single spruce stands
hung with usnea lichens, and small hawks circulate above, and
the chickadee lisps amid the evergreens, and the partridge and
rabbit skulk beneath; but now a more dismal and fitting day
dawns, and a different race of creatures awakes to express the
meaning of Nature there.

The Jays

AT LENGTH THE JAYS arrive, whose discordant screams were heard long before, as they were warily making their approach an eighth of a mile off, and in a stealthy and sneaking manner they flit from tree to tree, nearer and nearer, and pick up the kernels which the squirrels have dropped. Then, sitting on a pitch-pine bough, they attempt to swallow in their haste a kernel which is too big for their throats and chokes them; and after great labor they disgorge it, and spend an hour in the endeavor to crack it by repeated blows with their bills. They were manifestly thieves, and I had not much respect for them; but the squirrels, though at first shy, went to work as if they were taking what was their own.

Meanwhile also came the chickadees in flocks, which, picking up the crumbs the squirrels had dropped, flew to the nearest twig, and, placing them under their claws, hammered away at them with their little bills, as if it were an insect in the bark, till they were sufficiently reduced for their slender throats. A little flock of these titmice came daily to pick a dinner out of my woodpile, or the crumbs at my door, with faint flitting lisping notes, like the tinkling of icicles in the grass, or else with sprightly *day day day*, or more rarely, in springlike days, a wiry summery *phe-be* from the woodside. They were so familiar that at length one alighted on an armful of wood which I was carrying in, and pecked at the sticks without fear. I once had a sparrow alight upon my shoulder for a moment while I was hoeing in a village garden, and I felt that I was more distinguished by that circumstance than I should have been by any epaulet I could have worn. The squirrels also grew at last to be quite familiar, and occasionally stepped upon my shoe, when that was the nearest way.

The Laughter
of the Loon

IN THE FALL THE loon (*Colymbus glacialis*) came, as usual, to moult and bathe in the pond, making the woods ring with his wild laughter before I had risen. At rumor of his arrival all the Mill-dam sportsmen are on the alert, in gigs and on foot, two by two and three by three, with patent rifles and conical balls and spy-glasses. They come rustling through the woods like autumn leaves, at least ten men to one loon. Some station themselves on this side of the pond, some on that, for the poor bird cannot be omnipresent; if he dive here he must come up there. But now the kind October wind rises, rustling the leaves and rippling the surface of the water, so that no loon can be heard or seen, though his foes sweep the pond with spyglasses, and make the woods resound with their discharges. The waves generously rise and dash angrily, taking sides with all water-fowl, and our sportsmen must beat a retreat to town and shop and unfinished jobs. But they were too often successful. When

70

I went to get a pail of water early in the morning I frequently saw this stately bird sailing out of my cove within a few rods. If I endeavored to overtake him in a boat, in order to see how he would maneuver, he would dive and be completely lost, so that I did not discover him again, sometimes, till the latter part of the day. But I was more than a match for him on the surface. He commonly went off in a rain.

As I was paddling along the north shore one very calm October afternoon, for such days especially they settle onto the lakes, like the milkweed down, having looked in vain over the pond for a loon, suddenly one, sailing out from the shore toward the middle a few rods in front of me, set up his wild laugh and betrayed himself. I pursued with a paddle and he dived, but when he came up I was nearer than before. He dived again, but I miscalculated the direction he would take, and we were fifty rods apart when he came to the surface this time, for I had helped to widen the interval; and again he laughed long and loud, and with more reason than before. He maneuvered so cunningly that I could not get within half a dozen rods of him. Each time, when he came to the surface, turning his head this way and that, he coolly surveyed the water and the land, and apparently chose his course so that he might come up where there was the widest expense of water and at the greatest distance from the boat. It was surprising how quickly he made up his mind and put his resolve into execution. He led me at once to the widest part of the pond, and could not be driven from it. While he was thinking one thing in his brain, I was endeavoring to divine his thought in mine. It was a pretty game, played on the smooth surface of the pond, a man against a loon. Suddenly your adversary's checker disappears beneath the board, and the problem is to place yours nearest to where his will appear again. Sometimes he would come up unexpectedly on the opposite side of me, having apparently passed directly under the boat. So long-winded was he and so unweariable, that when he had swum farthest he would immediately plunge again, nevertheless; and then no wit could divine where in the deep pond, beneath the smooth surface, he might be speeding his way like a fish, for he had time and ability to visit the bottom of the pond in its deepest part. It is said that loons have been caught in the New York lakes eighty feet beneath the surface, with hooks set for trout—though Walden is deeper than that. How surprised must the fishes be to see this ungainly visitor from another sphere speeding his way amid their schools! Yet he appeared to know his course as surely under water as on the surface, and swam much faster there. Once or twice I saw a ripple where he approached the surface, just put his head out to reconnoiter, and instantly dived again. I found that it was as well for me to rest on my oars and wait his reappearing as to endeavor to calculate where he would rise; for again and again, when I was straining my eyes over the surface one way, I would suddenly be startled by his unearthly laugh behind me. But why, after displaying so much cunning, did he invariably betray himself the moment he came up by that loud laugh? Did not his white breast enough betray him? He was indeed a silly loon, I thought. I could commonly hear the splash of the water when he came up, and so also detected him. But after an hour he seemed as fresh as ever, dived as willingly, and swam yet farther than at first. It was surprising to see how serenely he sailed off with unruffled breast when he came to the surface, doing all the work with his webbed feet beneath. His usual note was this demoniac laughter, yet somewhat like that of a waterfowl; but occasionally, when he had balked me most successfully and come up a long way off, he uttered a long-drawn unearthly howl, probably more like that of a wolf than any bird; as when a beast puts his muzzle to the ground and deliberately howls. This was his looning, perhaps the wildest sound that is ever heard here, making the woods ring far and wide. I concluded that he laughed in derision of my efforts, confident of his own resources. Though the sky was by this time overcast, the pond was so smooth that I could see where he broke the surface when I did not hear him. His white breast, the stillness of the air, and the smoothness of the water were all against him. At length, having come up fifty rods off, he uttered one of those prolonged howls, as if calling on the god of loons to aid him, and immediately there came a wind from the east and rippled the surface, and filled the whole air with misty rain, and I was impressed as if it were the prayer of the loon answered, and his god was angry with me; and so I left him disappearing far away on the tumultuous surface.

Winter

AT LENGTH THE WINTER set in in good earnest, just as I had finished plastering, and the wind began to howl around the house as if it had not had permission to do so till then. Night after night the geese came lumbering in in the dark with a clangor and a whistling of wings, even after the ground was covered with snow, some to alight in Walden, and some flying low over the woods toward Fair Haven, bound for Mexico. Several times, when returning from the village at ten or eleven o'clock at night, I heard the tread of a flock of geese, or else ducks, on the dry leaves in the woods by a pond-hole behind my dwelling, where they had come up to feed, and the faint honk or quack of their leader as they hurried off. In 1845 Walden froze entirely over for the first time on the night of the 22d of December, Flints' and other shallower ponds and the river having been frozen ten days or more; in '46, the 16th; in '49, about the 31st; and in '50, about the 27th of December; in '52, the 5th of January; in '53, the 31st of December. The snow had already covered the ground since the 25th of November, and surrounded me suddenly with the scenery of winter. I withdrew yet farther into my shell, and endeavored to keep a bright fire both within my house and within my breast. My employment out of doors now was to collect the dead wood in the forest, bringing it in my hands or on my shoulders, or sometimes trailing a dead pine tree under each arm to my shed. An old forest fence which had seen its best days was a great haul for me. I sacrificed it to Vulcan, for it was past serving the god Terminus. How much more interesting an event is that man's supper who has just been forth in the snow to hunt, nay, you might say, steal, the fuel to cook it with! His bread and meat are sweet. There are enough fagots and waste wood of all kinds in the forests of most of our towns to support many fires, but which at present warm none, and, some think, hinder the growth of the young wood. There was also the driftwood of the pond. In the course of the summer I had discovered a raft of pitch-pine logs with the bark on, pinned together by the Irish when the railroad was built. This I hauled up partly on the shore. After soaking two years and then lying high six months it was perfectly sound, though waterlogged past drying. I amused myself one winter day with sliding this piecemeal across the pond, nearly half a mile, skating behind with one end of a log fifteen feet long on my shoulder, and the other on the ice; or I tied several logs together with a birch withe, and then, with a longer birch or alder which had a hook at the end, dragged them across. Though completely waterlogged and almost as heavy as lead, they not only burned long, but made a very hot fire; nay, I thought that they burned better for the soaking, as if the pitch, being confined by the water, burned longer as in a lamp.

The Ice

I ALSO HEARD THE whooping of the ice in the pond, my great bedfellow in that part of Concord, as if it were restless in its bed and would fain turn over, were troubled with flatulency and bad dreams; or I was waked by the cracking of the ground by the frost, as if some one had driven a team against my door, and in the morning would find a crack in the earth a quarter of a mile long and a third of an inch wide.

Sometimes I heard the foxes as they ranged over the snow crust, in moonlight nights, in search of a partridge or other game, barking raggedly and demoniacally like forest dogs, as if laboring with some anxiety, or seeking expression, struggling for light and to be dogs outright and run freely in the streets; for if we take the ages into our account, may there not be a civilization going on among brutes as well as men? They seemed to me to be rudimental, burrowing men, still standing on their defence, awaiting their transformation. Sometimes one came near to my window, attracted by my light, barked a vulpine curse at me, and then retreated.

A Sound of Wings

FOR SOUNDS IN WINTER nights, and often in winter days, I heard the forlorn but melodious note of a hooting owl indefinitely far; such a sound as the frozen earth would yield if struck with a suitable plectrum, the very *lingua vernacula* of Walden Wood, and quite familiar to me at last, though I never saw the bird while it was making it. I seldom opened my door in a winter evening without hearing it; *Hoo hoo hoo, hoorer hoo,* sounded sonorously, and the first three syllables accented somewhat like *how der do;* or sometimes *hoo hoo* only. One night in the beginning of winter, before the pond froze over, about nine o'clock, I was startled by the loud honking of a goose, and, stepping to the door, heard the sound of their wings like a tempest in the woods as they flew low over my house. They passed over the pond toward Fair Haven, seemingly deterred from settling by my light, their commodore honking all the while with a regular beat. Suddenly an unmistakable cat-owl from very near me, with the most harsh and tremendous voice I ever heard from any inhabitant of the woods, responded at regular intervals to the goose, as if determined to expose and disgrace this intruder from Hudson's Bay by exhibiting a greater compass and volume of voice in a native, and *boo-hoo* him out of Concord horizon. What do you mean by alarming the citadel at this time of night consecrated to me? Do you think I am ever caught napping at such an hour, and that I have not got lungs and a larynx as well as yourself? *Boo-hoo, boo-hoo, boo-hoo!* It was one of the most thrilling discords I ever heard. And yet, if you had a discriminating ear, there were in it the elements of a concord such as these plains never saw nor heard.

The Moles

THE MOLES NESTED IN my cellar, nibbling every third potato, and making a snug bed even there of some hair left after plastering and of brown paper; for even the wildest animals love comfort and warmth as well as man, and they survive the winter only because they are so careful to secure them. Some of my friends spoke as if I was coming to the woods on purpose to freeze myself. The animal merely makes a bed, which he warms with his body, in a sheltered place; but man, having discovered fire, boxes up some air in a spacious apartment, and warms that, instead of robbing himself, makes that his bed, in which he can move about divested of more cumbrous clothing, maintain a kind of summer in the midst of winter, and by means of windows even admit the light, and with a lamp lengthen out the day. Thus he goes a step or two beyond instinct, and saves a little time for the fine arts. Though, when I had been exposed to the rudest blasts a long time, my whole body began to grow torpid, when I reached the genial atmosphere of my house I soon recovered my faculties and prolonged my life. But the most luxuriously housed has little to boast of in this respect, nor need we trouble ourselves to speculate how the human race may be at last destroyed. It would be easy to cut their threads any time with a little sharper blast from the north. We go on dating from Cold Fridays and Great Snows; but a little colder Friday, or greater snow, would put a period to man's existence on the globe.

Melting

WALDEN IS MELTING APACE. There is a canal two rods wide along the northerly and westerly sides, and wider still at the east end. A great field of ice has cracked off from the main body. I hear a song-sparrow singing from the bushes on the shore—*olit, olit, olit—chip, chip, chip, che char—che wiss, wiss, wiss.* He too is helping to crack it. How handsome the great sweeping curves in the edge of the ice, answering somewhat to those of the shore, but more regular! It is unusually hard, owing to the recent severe but transient cold, and all watered or waved like a palace floor. But the wind slides eastward over its opaque surface in vain, till it reaches the living surface beyond. It is glorious to behold this ribbon of water sparkling in the sun, the bare face of the pond full of glee and youth, as if it spoke the joy of the fishes within it, and of the sands on its shore—a silvery sheen as from the scales of a *leuciscus*, as it were all one active fish. Such is the contrast between winter and spring. Walden was dead and is alive again.

The Deck of the World

IN THE MORNING I watched the geese from the door through the mist, sailing in the middle of the pond, fifty rods off, so large and tumultuous that Walden appeared like an artificial pond for their amusement. But when I stood on the shore they at once rose up with a great flapping of wings at the signal of their commander, and when they had got into rank circled about over my head, twenty-nine of them, and then steered straight to Canada, with a regular *honk* from the leader at intervals, trusting to break their fast in muddier pools. A "plump" of ducks rose at the same time and took the route to the north in the wake of their noisier cousins.

For a week I heard the circling groping clangor of some solitary goose in the foggy mornings, seeking its companion, and still peopling the woods with the sound of a larger life than they could sustain. In April the pigeons were seen again flying express in small flocks, and in due time I heard the martins twittering over my clearing, though it had not seemed that the township contained so many that it could afford me any, and I fancied that they were peculiarly of the ancient race that dwelt in hollow trees ere white men came. In almost all climes the tortoise and the frog are among the precursors and heralds of this season, and birds fly with song and glancing plumage, and plants spring and bloom, and winds blow, to correct this slight oscillation of the poles and preserve the equilibrium of Nature.

As every season seems best to us in its turn, so the coming in of spring is like the creation of Cosmos out of Chaos and the realization of the Golden Age.

82

The Sun Is
But a Morning Star

EVERY ONE HAS HEARD the story which has gone the rounds of New England, of a strong and beautiful bug which came out of the dry leaf of an old table of apple-tree wood, which had stood in a farmer's kitchen for sixty years, first in Connecticut, and afterward in Massachusetts—from an egg deposited in the living tree many years earlier still, as appeared by counting the annual layers beyond it; which was heard gnawing out for several weeks, hatched perchance by the heat of an urn. Who does not feel his faith in a resurrection and immortality strengthened by hearing of this? Who knows what beautiful and winged life, whose egg has been buried for ages under many concentric layers of woodenness in the dead dry life of society, deposited at first in the alburnum of the green and living tree, which has been gradually converted into the semblance of its well-seasoned tomb—heard perchance gnawing out now for years by the astonished family of man, as they sat round the festive board—may unexpectedly come forth from amidst society's most trivial and hand-selled furniture, to enjoy its perfect summer life at last!

I do not say that John or Jonathan will realize all this; but such is the character of that morrow which mere lapse of time can never make to dawn. The light which puts out our eyes is darkness to us. Only that day dawns to which we are awake. There is more day to dawn. The sun is but a morning star.

To See the Spring Come In

ONE ATTRACTION IN COMING to the woods to live was that I should have leisure and opportunity to see the Spring come in. The ice in the pond at length begins to be honeycombed, and I can set my heel in it as I walk. Fogs and rains and warmer suns are gradually melting the snow; the days have grown sensibly longer; and I see how I shall get through the winter without adding to my woodpile, for large fires are no longer necessary. I am on the alert for the first signs of spring, to hear the chance note of some arriving bird, or the striped squirrel's chirp, for his stores must be now nearly exhausted, or see the woodchuck venture out of his winter quarters. On the 13th of March, after I had heard the bluebird, song-sparrow, and red-wing, the ice was still nearly a foot thick. As the weather grew warmer it was not sensibly worn away by the water, nor broken up and floated off as in rivers, but, though it was completely melted for half a rod in width about the shore, the middle was merely honeycombed and saturated with water, so that you could put your foot through it when six inches thick; but by the next day evening, perhaps, after a warm rain followed by fog, it would have wholly disappeared, all gone off with the fog, spirited away. One year I went across the middle only five days before it disappeared entirely. In 1845 Walden was first completely open on the 1st of April; in '46, the 25th of March; in '47, the 8th of April; in '51, the 28th of March; in '52, the 18th of April; in '53, the 23d of March; in '54, about the 7th of April.

84

A Different Drummer

SOME ARE DINNING IN our ears that we Americans, and moderns generally, are intellectual dwarfs compared with the ancients, or even the Elizabethan men. But what is that to the purpose? A living dog is better than a dead lion. Shall a man go and hang himself because he belongs to the race of pygmies, and not be the biggest pygmy that he can? Let everyone mind his own business, and endeavor to be what he was made.

Why should we be in such desperate haste to succeed and in such desperate enterprises? If a man does not keep pace with his companions, perhaps it is because he hears a different drummer. Let him step to the music which he hears, however measured or far away.

To Travel the Only Path I Can

I DELIGHT TO COME to my bearings—not walk in procession with pomp and parade, in a conspicuous place, but to walk even with the Builder of the universe, if I may—not to live in this restless, nervous, bustling, trivial nineteenth century, but stand or sit thoughtfully while it goes by. What are men celebrating? They are all on a committee of arrangements, and hourly expect a speech from somebody. God is only the president of the day, and Webster is his orator. I love to weigh, to settle, to gravitate toward that which most strongly and rightfully attracts me; not hang by the beam of the scale and try to weigh less, not suppose a case, but take the case that is; to travel the only path I can, and that on which no power can resist me. It affords me no satisfaction to commence to spring an arch before I have got a solid foundation.

Drive a Nail Home

ONLY WHAT IS THOUGHT, said, or done at a certain rare coincidence is good. I would not be one of those who will foolishly drive a nail into mere lath and plastering; such a deed would keep me awake nights. Give me a hammer, and let me feel for the furrowing. Do not depend on the putty. Drive a nail home and clinch it so faithfully that you can wake up in the night and think of your work with satisfaction—a work at which you would not be ashamed to invoke the Muse. So will help you God, and so only. Every nail driven should be as another rivet in the machine of the universe, you carrying on the work.

87

Part Two

AD ASTRA

Genius

IN LITERATURE IT IS only the wild that attracts us. Dullness is but another name for tameness. It is the uncivilized free and wild thinking in Hamlet and the Iliad, in all the scriptures and mythologies, not learned in the schools, that delights us. As the wild duck is more swift and beautiful than the tame, so is the wild—the mallard—thought, which 'mid falling dews wings its way above the fens. A truly good book is something as natural, and as unexpectedly and unaccountably fair and perfect, as a wild-flower discovered on the prairies of the West or in the jungles of the East. Genius is a light which makes the darkness visible, like the lightning's flash, which perchance shatters the temple of knowledge itself—and not a taper lighted at the hearthstone of the race, which pales before the light of common day.

Wild and Free

IN SHORT, ALL GOOD things are wild and free. There is something in a strain of music, whether produced by an instrument or by the human voice—take the sound of a bugle in a summer night, for instance—which by its wildness, to speak without satire, reminds me of the cries emitted by wild beasts in their native forests. It is so much of their wildness as I can understand. Give me for my friends and neighbors wild men, not tame ones. The wildness of the savage is but a faint symbol of the awful ferity with which good men and lovers meet.

I love even to see the domestic animals reassert their native rights—any evidence that they have not wholly lost their original wild habits and vigor; as when my neighbor's cow breaks out of her pasture early in the spring and boldly swims the river, a cold, gray tide, twenty-five or thirty rods wide, swollen by the melted snow. It is the buffalo crossing the Mississippi. This exploit confers some dignity on the herd in my eyes—already dignified. The seeds of instinct are preserved under the thick hides of cattle and horses, like seeds in the bowels of the earth, an indefinite period.

Business

LET US CONSIDER THE WAY in which we spend our lives.

This world is a place of business. What an infinite bustle! I am awaked almost every night by the panting of the locomotive. It interrupts my dreams. There is no sabbath. It would be glorious to see mankind at leisure for once. It is nothing but work, work, work. I cannot easily buy a blankbook to write thoughts in; they are commonly ruled for dollars and cents. An Irishman, seeing me making a minute in the fields, took it for granted that I was calculating my wages. If a man was tossed out of a window when an infant, and so made a cripple for life, or scared out of his wits by the Indians, it is regretted chiefly because he was thus incapacitated for—business! I think that there is nothing, not even crime, more opposed to poetry, to philosophy, ay, to life itself, than this incessant business.

With Respect to My Freedom

PERHAPS I AM MORE than usually jealous with respect to my freedom. I feel that my connection with and obligation to society are still very slight and transient. Those slight labors which afford me a livelihood, and by which it is allowed that I am to some extent serviceable to my contemporaries, are as yet commonly a pleasure to me, and I am not often reminded that they are a necessity. So far I am successful. But I foresee that if my wants should be much increased, the labor required to supply them would become a drudgery. If I should sell both my forenoons and afternoons to society, as most appear to do, I am sure that for me there would be nothing left worth living for. I trust that I shall never thus sell my birthright for a mess of pottage. I wish to suggest that a man may be very industrious, and yet not spend his time well. There is no more fatal blunderer than he who consumes the greater part of his life getting his living. All great enterprises are self-supporting. The poet, for instance, must sustain his body by his poetry, as a steam planing-mill feeds its boilers with the shavings it makes. You must get your living by loving. But as it is said of the merchants that ninety-seven in a hundred fail, so the life of men generally, tried by this standard, is a failure, and bankruptcy may be surely prophesied.

For Love of It

THE AIM OF THE laborer should be, not to get his living, to get "a good job," but to perform well a certain work; and, even in a pecuniary sense, it would be economy for a town to pay its laborers so well that they would not feel that they were working for low ends, as for a livelihood merely, but for scientific, or even moral ends. Do not hire a man who does your work for money, but him who does it for love of it.

Read Not the Times

THERE IS INSPIRATION, THAT gossip which comes to the ear of the attentive mind from the courts of heaven. There is the profane and stale revelation of the barroom and the police court. The same ear is fitted to receive both communications. Only the character of the hearer determines to which it shall be open, and to which closed. I believe that the mind can be permanently profaned by the habit of attending to trivial things, so that all our thoughts shall be tinged with triviality. Our very intellect shall be macadamized, as it were, its foundation broken into fragments for the wheels of travel to roll over; and if you would know what will make the most durable pavement, surpassing rolled stones, spruce blocks, and asphaltum, you have only to look into some of our minds which have been subjected to this treatment so long.

If we have thus desecrated ourselves—as who has not?—the remedy will be by wariness and devotion to reconsecrate ourselves, and make once more a fane of the mind. We should treat our minds, that is, ourselves, as innocent and ingenuous children, whose guardians we are, and be careful what objects and what subjects we thrust on their attention. Read not the Times. Read the Eternities.

A Corporation
with a Conscience

AFTER ALL, THE PRACTICAL reason why, when the power is once in the hands of the people, a majority are permitted, and for a long period continue, to rule is not because they are most likely to be in the right, nor because this seems fairest to the minority, but because they are physically the strongest. But a government in which the majority rule in all cases cannot be based on justice, even as far as men understand it. Can there not be a government in which majorities do not virtually decide right and wrong, but conscience?—in which majorities decide only those questions to which the rule of expediency is applicable? Must the citizen ever for a moment, or in the least degree, resign his conscience to the legislator? Why has every man a conscience, then? I think that we should be men first, and subjects afterward. It is not desirable to cultivate a respect for the law, so much as for the right. The only obligation which I have a right to assume is to do at any time what I think right. It is truly enough said that a corporation has no conscience; but a corporation of conscientious men is a corporation *with* a conscience.

The True Place
for a Just Man

UNDER A GOVERNMENT WHICH imprisons any unjustly, the true place for a just man is also a prison. The proper place today, the only place which Massachusetts has provided for her freer and less desponding spirits, is in her prisons, to be put out and locked out of the State by her own act, as they have already put themselves out by their principles. It is there that the fugitive slave, and the Mexican prisoner on parole, and the Indian come to plead the wrongs of his race should find them; on that separate, but more free and honorable, ground, where the State places those who are not *with* her, but *against* her—the only house in a slave State in which a free man can abide with honor. If any think that their influence would be lost there, and their voices no longer afflict the ear of the State, that they would not be as an enemy within its walls, they do not know by how much truth is stronger than error, nor how much more eloquently and effectively he can combat injustice who has experienced a little in his own person. Cast your whole vote, not a strip of paper merely, but your whole influence. A minority is powerless while it conforms to the majority; it is not even a minority then; but it is irresistible when it clogs by its whole weight. If the alternative is to keep all just men in prison, or give up war and slavery, the State will not hesitate which to choose. If a thousand men were not to pay their tax-bills this year, that would not be a violent and bloody measure, as it would be to pay them, and enable the State to commit violence and shed innocent blood. This is, in fact, the definition of a peaceable revolution, if any such is possible. If the tax-gatherer, or any other public officer, asks me, as one has done, "But what shall I do?" my answer is, "If you really wish to do anything, resign your office." When the subject has refused allegiance, and the officer has resigned his office, then the revolution is accomplished. But even suppose blood should flow. Is there not a sort of blood shed when the conscience is wounded? Through this wound a man's real manhood and immortality flow out, and he bleeds to an everlasting death. I see this blood flowing now.

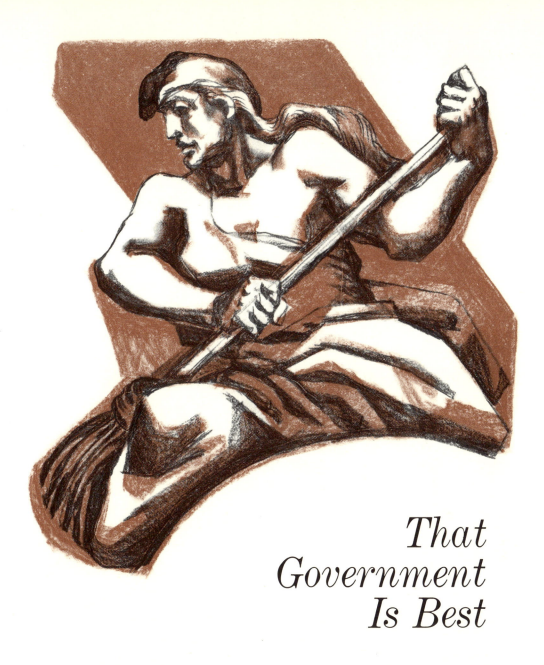

That Government Is Best

I HEARTILY ACCEPT THE motto, "That government is best which governs least"; and I should like to see it acted up to more rapidly and systematically. Carried out, it finally amounts to this, which also I believe—"That government is best which governs not at all"; and when men are prepared for it, that will be the kind of government which they will have.

Force

I HAVE PAID NO poll-tax for six years. I was put into a jail once on this account, for one night; and, as I stood considering the walls of solid stone, two or three feet thick, the door of wood and iron, a foot thick, and the iron grating which strained the light, I could not help being struck with the foolishness of that institution which treated me as if I were mere flesh and blood and bones, to be locked up. I wondered that it should have concluded at length that this was the best use it could put me to, and had never thought to avail itself of my services in some way. I saw that, if there was a wall of stone between me and my townsmen, there was a still more difficult one to climb or break through before they could get to be as free as I was. I did not for a moment feel confined, and the walls seemed a great waste of stone and mortar. I felt as if I alone of all my townsmen had paid my tax. They plainly did not know how to treat me, but behaved like persons who are underbred. In every threat and in every compliment there was a blunder; for they thought that my chief desire was to stand the other side of that stone wall. I could not but smile to see how industriously they locked the door on my meditations, which followed them out again without let or hindrance, and *they* were really all that was dangerous. As they could not reach me, they had resolved to punish my body; just as boys, if they cannot come at some person against whom they have a spite, will abuse his dog. I saw that the State was half-witted, that it was timid as a lone woman with her silver spoons, and that it did not know its friends from its foes, and I lost all my remaining respect for it, and pitied it.

Thus the State never intentionally confronts a man's sense, intellectual or moral, but only his body, his senses. It is not armed with superior wit or honesty, but with superior physical strength. I was not born to be forced. I will breathe after my own fashion. Let us see who is the strongest. What force has a multitude? They only can force me who obey a higher law than I. They force me to become like themselves. I do not hear of *men* being *forced* to live this way or that by masses of men. What sort of life were that to live? When I meet a government which says to me, "Your money or your life," why should I be in haste to give it my money? It may be in a great strait, and not know what to do: I cannot help that. It must help itself; do as I do. It is not worth the while to snivel about it. I am not responsible for the successful working of the machinery of society. I am not the son of the engineer. I perceive that, when an acorn and a chestnut fall side by side, the one does not remain inert to make way for the other, but both obey their own laws, and spring and grow and flourish as best they can, till one, perchance, overshadows and destroys the other. If a plant cannot live according to its nature, it dies; and so a man.

My Prisons

THE NIGHT IN PRISON was novel and interesting enough. The prisoners in their shirtsleeves were enjoying a chat and the evening air in the doorway, when I entered. But the jailer said, "Come, boys, it is time to lock up"; and so they dispersed, and I heard the sound of their steps returning into the hollow apartments. My roommate was introduced to me by the jailer as "a first-rate fellow and a clever man." When the door was locked, he showed me where to hang my hat, and how he managed matters there. The rooms were whitewashed once a month; and this one, at least, was the whitest, most simply furnished, and probably the neatest apartment in the town. He naturally wanted to know where I came from, and what brought me there; and, when I had told him, I asked him in my turn how he came there, presuming him to be an honest man, of course; and, as the world goes, I believe he was. "Why," said he, "they accuse me of burning a barn; but I never did it." As near as I could discover, he had probably gone to bed in a barn when drunk, and smoked his pipe there; and so a barn was burnt. He had the reputation of being a clever man, and had been there some three months waiting for his trial to come on, and would have to wait as much longer; but he was quite domesticated and contented, since he got his board for nothing, and thought that he was well treated.

He occupied one window, and I the other; and I saw that if one stayed there long, his principal business would be to look out the window. I had soon read all the tracts that were left there, and examined where former prisoners had broken out, and where a grate had been sawed off, and heard the history of the various occupants of that room; for I found that even here there was a history and a gossip which never circulated beyond the walls of the jail. Probably this is the only house in the town where verses are composed, which are afterward printed in a circular form, but not published. I was shown quite a long list of verses which were composed by some young men who had been detected in an attempt to escape, who avenged themselves by singing them.

I pumped my fellow-prisoner as dry as I could, for fear I should never see him again; but at length he showed me which was my bed, and left me to blow out the lamp.

It was like traveling into a far country, such as I had never expected to behold, to lie there for one night. It seemed to me that I never had heard the town clock strike before, nor the evening sounds of the village; for we slept with the windows open, which were inside the grating. It was to see my native village in the light of the Middle Ages, and our Concord was turned into a Rhine stream, and visions of knights and castles passed before me. They were the voices of old burghers that I heard in the streets. I was an involuntary spectator and auditor of whatever was done and said in the kitchen of the adjacent village inn—a wholly new and rare experience to me. It was a closer view of my native town. I was fairly inside of it. I never had seen its institutions before. This is one of its peculiar institutions; for it is a shire town. I began to comprehend what its inhabitants were about.

In the morning, our breakfasts were put through the hole in the door, in small oblong-square tin pans, made to fit, and holding a pint of chocolate, with brown bread, and an iron spoon. When they called for the vessels again, I was green enough to return what bread I had left; but my comrade seized it, and said that I should lay that up for lunch or dinner. Soon after he was let out to work at haying in a neighboring field, whither he went every day, and would not be back till noon; so he bade me good-day, saying that he doubted if he should see me again.

When I came out of prison—for some one interfered, and paid that tax—I did not perceive that great changes had taken place on the common, such as he observed who went in a youth and emerged a tottering and gray-headed man; and yet a change had to my eyes come over the scene—the town, and State, and country—greater than any that mere time could effect. I saw yet more distinctly the State in which I lived. I saw to what extent the people among whom I lived could be trusted as good neighbors and friends; that their friendship was for summer weather only; that they did not greatly pro-pose to do right; that they were a distinct race from me by their prejudices and superstitions, as the Chinamen and Malays are; that in their sacrifices to humanity they ran no risks, not even to their property; that after all they were not so noble

106

but they treated the thief as he had treated them, and hoped, by a certain outward observance and a few prayers, and by walking in a particular straight though useless path from time to time, to save their souls. This may be to judge my neighbors harshly; for I believe that many of them are not aware that they have such an institution as the jail in their village.

It was formerly the custom in our village, when a poor debtor came out of jail, for his acquaintances to salute him, looking through their fingers, which were crossed to represent the grating of a jail window, "How do ye do?" My neighbors did not thus salute me, but first looked at me, and then at one another, as if I had returned from a long journey. I was put into jail as I was going to the shoemaker's to get a shoe which was mended. When I was let out the next morning, I proceeded to finish my errand, and, having put on my mended shoe, joined a huckleberry party, who were impatient to put themselves under my conduct; and in half an hour—for the horse was soon tackled—was in the midst of a huckleberry field, on one of our highest hills, two miles off, and then the State was nowhere to be seen.

This is the whole history of "My Prisons."

Conformity

I DO NOT WISH to quarrel with any man or nation. I do not wish to split hairs, to make fine distinctions, or set myself up as better than my neighbors. I seek rather, I may say, even an excuse for conforming to the laws of the land. I am but too ready to conform to them. Indeed, I have reason to suspect myself on this head; and each year, as the tax-gatherer comes round, I find myself disposed to review the acts and position of the general and State governments, and the spirit of the people, to discover a pretext for conformity.

> "We must affect our country as our parents,
>   And if at any time we alienate
>   Our love or industry from doing it honor,
>   We must respect effects and teach the soul
>   Matter of conscience and religion,
>   And not desire of rule or benefit."

I believe that the State will soon be able to take all my work of this sort out of my hands, and then I shall be no better a patriot than my fellow-countrymen. Seen from a lower point of view, the Constitution, with all its faults, is very good; the law and the courts are very respectable; even this State and this American government are, in many respects, very admirable, and rare things, to be thankful for, such as a great many have described them; but seen from a point of view a little higher, they are what I have described them; seen from a higher still, and the highest, who shall say what they are, or that they are worth looking at or thinking of at all?

Long Ago
I Lost a Hound

I LONG AGO LOST a hound, a bay horse, and a turtledove, and am still on their trail. Many are the travelers I have spoken concerning them, describing their tracks and what calls they answered to. I have met one or two who had heard the hound, and the tramp of the horse, and even seen the dove disappear behind a cloud, and they seemed as anxious to recover them as if they had lost them themselves.

111

Thoreau's companions in the drawing on page 110 are Ralph Waldo Emerson, who was his earliest influence; Bronson Alcott, his most congenial spirit; and John Brown, who was his greatest hero. What Thoreau meant by his lost bay horse, hound, and dove will always remain a fascinating subject for individual interpretation.

J. D.